·FANCIFUL NIGHTS·

·FANCIFUL NIGHTS·

TOMEK • HANNA • MILTON

SeTo
PUBLISHING

SeTo Publishing
Apartment D, 11 Whitaker Place
Auckland, New Zealand

Concept and photography by Tomek Sikora
Artwork and bestiary by Grant Hanna
Text by Ivan Milton

ISBN 0 908697 32 5

Printed in Hong Kong by Everbest Printing Co. Ltd.

·FANCIFUL NIGHTS·

grateful thanks to:
Ania, Alek, Chloe, David, Jeff, Jessie, Kaja, Kasia,
Leon, Maciek, Maks, Malgosia, Mateuse, Matthew,
Marta, Michal, Nina, Ola, Tamara, Tom and York.

Fanciful Nights

In the dark, and as the city sleeps,
Through the window, in between the sheets
This really is the greatest place to meet,
At night, when they are both asleep.

A dragon and a flying Teddy Bear
Of course, and Snabbit too is there.
It's fun and games that they are here to share,
Tonight, when dreams are in the air.

Bicycle Bird

Dream of a Ragamuffin man.
He whispers things you've never heard,
He has a truly wondrous plan
How to catch a bicycle bird.

We went along to where he led,
And found a rainbow in the mist.
But then he simply looked and said,
"A bicycle bird just doesn't exist."

The Butterflies' Birthday

Can butterflies have birthdays,
Or was it just a dream?
Is that the way a trumpet plays,
And are things what they seem?

No! That's a warning elves will make,
With butterflies about,
Who'll sit and eat our birthday cake,
To stop us getting stout.

Rabbit Rider

A gentleman from England and
a princess from Afghanistan,
Were chased across the desert sand
they ran and ran and ran and ran.

It was a frog who hoped
(he was a prince you see)
To kiss this Eastern princess and
he thought he would be free.

But someone magic saw
and sent a special fog.
He missed the kiss and must remain
a rabbit ridden frog.

Reading Teddy

I've tried to make my Teddy read,
I dressed him in a suit and tie,
I tried my magic,
Tried to plead,
He just won't read
no matter how I try.

But then last night
he rose up in his chair,
He waved his paw and
said I wasn't fair,
He laughed and said that
he would leave the house
If he must read and
not my old pet mouse.

Snabbit

What a bad dream!
To be caught in a tree,
With a Snabbit around,
Waiting to see,
If you drop to the ground.

But when the worst comes,
And you fall in the arms,
Of a wriggling, slithering Snabbit,
Don't worry too much,
For to tickle your toes,
Is really his only bad habit.

The Riddle Dragon

It was a dragon that we saw,
Playing on the floor.
He wasn't breathing fire,
but just for fun
Was telling riddles one by one.

Now when a soldier answers wrong,
A puff of smoke and he is gone.
So we must answer loud and clear,
And make that dragon disappear.

A Land of Elephants and Mice

A strange policeman drove us home,
And where were we do you suppose?
For in the car was only room,
For him and his peculiar nose.

A land of elephants and mice,
You can get home but for a price.
For only elephants can drive of course,
And only mice can open doors.

The Collector

My beautiful dragonflies,
The girls were just their size.
They wanted them alive these two,
For their little human zoo.

But what a trick we played,
It was a trap I laid.
And now they sit and pass the time
In an insect zoo of mine!

Free Wheeler

It was summer in the wild fire,
Shades of summer rising higher,
Reaching for the long hot blue,
Reaching out for me and you.

My free wheeler skating home,
Or just a zebra all alone,
Who in the power of his stare,
Makes flames of summer reappear.

Flying Penguin

Please don't be misled,
He is a penguin like he said.
Who really finds it hard to be,
A bird with wings who likes to ski.

So please don't laugh into his face,
Just because he lost the race,
For even those who cannot fly,
Should really have the right to try.

Ode to a Vulture

Near the town, she floated down,
Above the ground, without a sound,
She lightly rose, upon her toes.
But when she sang, her sad voice rang,
With such a note, so full of hope,
That now we see, how she can be,
A dainty dancing vulture too.

Super Bear

What does it mean,
When you wake in the night
at a quarter to two,
Ready for school
and with nothing to do?

What does it mean,
When you watch the TV
just to fill in time,
And before too long
its a quarter to nine?

What does it mean
When a bear in a cape
flies out of the screen?
What does it mean?!
It means it's a dream, that's all.
You're asleep in bed, late for school!